TALLER THAN BEFORE

Other Orchard Storybooks

A CLIPPER STREET STORY

TALLER THAN BEFORE

Bernard Ashley

Illustrated by
Jane Cope

ORCHARD BOOKS
London

Text copyright © Bernard Ashley 1987
Illustrations copyright © Jane Cope 1987
First published in Great Britain in 1987 by
ORCHARD BOOKS
10 Golden Square, London W1R 3AF
Orchard Books Australia
14 Mars Road, Lane Cove NSW 2066
Orchard Books Canada
20 Torbay Road, Markham, Ontario 23P 1G6
1 85213 076 8
Printed in Great Britain
by A. Wheaton, Exeter

The Clipper Street stories are set
in and around the Greenwich area
of South East London which is
shown on the map overleaf.

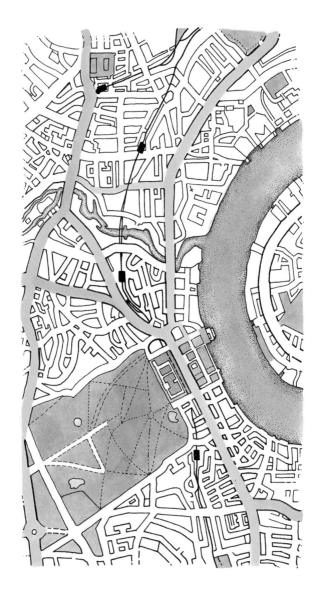

CHAPTER
ONE

Roberta Richards was the one they always asked. When a job needed doing at Regent Primary the teachers always sent for her. If a special visitor was being given a good impression they'd get her to bring out her work.

And if it was a note going round they knew she wouldn't forget anyone and miss out any of the classes. They knew she could read it but still they didn't mind. She'd smile a bit at their jokes but they trusted her. And they counted the days they'd still have her because they liked her—even the other children.

Her mother had been the same, she was

always telling Roberta: a born monitor who worked hard at her lessons and at her acting. Now she was getting known on the telly and was being spotted in the street. Nearly-famous, so it was worth all the effort. And already Roberta was on the way to being a good violinist, with her extra lessons at school.

Over at Clipper Primary, Slade Bendix was the one they always *didn't* ask. At least, not for jobs or going out of anyone's sight. When a child needed first aid they might ask him because he'd probably caused it. But otherwise they just sat on him and tried to get him to be better behaved, counting the weeks till he moved on.

From his first ever day, when he plopped the wet sand through the slit in Mrs Perritt's guitar, he'd been marked. And from that same first day others had been marked by him. He soon learned to see to that.

His father hadn't been any different, he

reckoned. But a regular dose of the cane
had done him the world of good, he always
said. Now he ran the "Yard Arm" pub in

Clipper Street, and there weren't many people who stepped out of line in there. They knew where they stood. They were all as good as gold and they laughed at Slade's little tricks because his dad was the guv'nor.

And the boy washed glasses and emptied ashtrays as if he'd been doing it all his life. Which he had, very nearly.

CHAPTER
TWO

Everyone said music festivals weren't meant to be competitions between schools. But they were, and most of the children knew it. The teachers at the side of the stage smiled and clapped hard at everything: but it was hard and long for their own schools, hard and short for all the others.

And there was no doubt about what the word "pride" meant for people who saw the looks on the headteachers' faces in the audience. On those nights music was meant to be the only winner—but there was still a lot of glory being chased around the old Town Hall.

Roberta Richards didn't need telling how much her teachers depended on her: how she was their star that night, the image of the school. If she'd had her violin tuned by Mrs Palfrey once she'd had it plucked up at the teacher's ear a dozen times. And she'd heard them fixing to have a special spotlight on her for her solo. The school choir sang O.K., but hers was the item where there wouldn't be a cool pair of hands in the house. Variations on *Shenandoah* arranged for violin. A slow shanty in a white dress lit by a sharp blue spot. It should be magic.

Over at the side of the stage, next to go on after the solo, a group from Clipper School was being kept quiet. It was mostly fingers at lips but Slade Bendix was having to have his hand held hard.

No one could shake a pair of maracas in time like Slade, so that's what he'd be doing. But cracking them on heads wasn't in the item. Nor was shaking them up skirts, not even in perfect time, and that's what he'd done at rehearsal. So the Clipper School head was the one who *wasn't* in the audience, being definitely on duty backstage in case a couple of maracas needed muffling.

Over on her side Roberta stood still and took in some deep breaths. With an actress for a mother she knew about nerves and how you had to have them.

"Nerves are high-bred horses," her mother always said. "Just get 'em in harness and you go along fine!" Oxygen did that—and it helped to get rid of that nervous need to go to the toilet. But nothing could calm the excitement.

For Roberta that night there was something else, besides. In with the nerves and the performance feeling there was this other excitement—although it was buried deeper right now. That night she'd be sleeping in a new bed in a new room of her own. She'd gone to school from her old place in Deptford and she'd be going home to a new house in Clipper Street. And that wasn't something you did any old day of the week.

She'd sat at rehearsal that afternoon thinking how today was definitely one of those days when everything happened. There'd be no more Clarice sharing her room to boss her what to do. There'd be no more staring up at the tuckings-in of that top bunk, because tonight she'd be seeing the ceiling. Tonight was the sort of night you just looked forward to—and didn't look beyond.

14

pleasure went on lifting her up. She was like a glider on warm air. No mistakes. She'd pleased Mrs Palfrey, and the head; and she knew her parents wouldn't be disappointed, either.

This time the applause was hard and long—from everyone. Some clapped above their heads; and a few got their handkerchiefs out. Roberta took it the way actors

do, her arms hanging straight, violin in one hand, bow in the other—and she gave just a modest nod of the head before the blue spot snapped off.

"Roberta, that was great! Well done! Whatever's the school going to do without you?"

Walking off, Roberta didn't mind. She was floating high above any problem tonight. She was suddenly jostled by the Clipper children rushing on, but she felt nothing of that. She didn't even hear Slade Bendix as he was hustled away.

"Pouf!" he said to her, before a big hand went over his mouth. All Roberta knew was the feel of success. She'd done well and she was wanted. Her parents' faces were going to be something really special to see. And you can't buy any of that in the shops!

Besides which, tonight she'd be sleeping in Clipper Street. In her own room at last. The world was a marvellous place. Not even rude kids from strange schools could change that, could they?

a different name. Well, it shouldn't be all that different, should it?

But it was. It was very different. This school was tall, with turrets; and it was even hard to find the way in. The first staircase they came to went up to an empty hall near the top, and then by the time they'd found the head's room and had Roberta enrolled, Mrs Richards needed help to find the way out. But that wasn't all. This school had a whole different feel to it. People went past her without a hello. All the doors seemed to be shut very tight. And there were *other* people walking round with the notes.

Within ten minues of going in through the gate she was sitting at a table in class, and not very happy. Her new teacher had forced a smile when she'd been taken in, but he'd made a big fuss of finding room for her to sit. And when she did, it was at the only spare seat in the room, next to some-one who usually sat on his own.

Slade Bendix. The boy from the night before.

The class eyed her up. She ignored their smirks. She tried to tell herself they were only coughing behind their hands. But she didn't like it. She just wasn't used to being talked about as if she were some sort of novelty. And this kid next to her, she thought: he was going to be trouble. Just the way he looked at her, the way he lay with his head on his arm, staring at her. It wasn't a look which said they were going to be the best of friends.

And the way the teacher talked. . . . It was great for the others because he had nicknames for them: he called this boy next to her *Trouble*. But he didn't even give her *Roberta*. When he asked her something it was all straight, like a bus conductor demanding the ticket money. Not nasty; but then not nice, either.

No, Clipper Primary was definitely not a home from home, nor a school from school.

And Roberta started thinking about Regent and what her old class would be doing. If she closed her eyes she could see Mrs Palfrey's special smile—and only being very strong about it stopped her eyes from starting to prickle.

There was just this feeling in the air that something unpleasant would happen. And when it did it was over space, the sharing of space. Suddenly the very thing which Roberta had got sorted out at her new home reared up to hurt her at her new school.

Slade Bendix wasn't used to being cramped. For years he'd been given a wide berth in school, double room to spread his hard hands and his active feet. Accidents had been more or less ruled out by putting no one near enough to him to be knocked. Now the new girl was there to share his space till the seats got sorted out.

And what new girl was this? His face was twisted up, even thinking the question.

She might be in different clothes from last night, but he'd know that snobby face anywhere. It was that black kid with the violin he'd wanted to put his foot through.

His face took on a calm, dreamy look. Smash the thing to bits! See her get a clap at the end then! She wouldn't have done a bow, she'd have screamed her head off.

He reared himself up.

"Get over!" he told her. Her elbow was

halfway—but halfway was his space, same as the rest was, too. "Go on!" He punched her hard, and hurt her. Made her move it.

"Don't you do that!" she hissed at him. "Get over your own!" And she elbowed him back from her side.

Which was all Slade Bendix wanted. He scraped back his chair and slapped her hard round the head.

"Don' you 'it me!" he shouted. "Cow!" And he hit her again, went for her as if he'd go through her.

"Stop that! Stop that! Slade Bendix!" Mr Ransom was over from the blackboard fast, pulling the boy off Roberta and holding up his wrist like a winner.

Slade Bendix stopped. He stood and just snarled.

"Look what she done!" he complained, pulling up a sleeve to show the red on his arm.

"What's this? What's this?" Mr Ransom turned on Roberta.

But Roberta stood her ground. Her head hurt, but she was more in shock than in pain.

"You done it first!" she gave the boy, direct. "You started it."

"To me! To me! Talk to me!" the teacher told her in a fast voice. "Tell *me* what happened."

But now Roberta couldn't find the words to talk to him. It seemed so babyish, what had happened. This wasn't what she was used to with Mrs Palfrey. And how could the bloke be just as shouting with her as he was with this monster kid? All she could do—and she found herself doing it—was fold her arms, take deep breaths, and stare the man in the face.

"Sit there!" Mr Ransom dragged a chair into a space miles from anyone and sat Slade Bendix on it. "Sit there and don't move!" He turned to Roberta again. "And you sit down and get on with your work!" She didn't move. "Go on!"

Swallowing something hard in her throat Roberta did as she was told.

"And don't you come the little madam with me, I'll tell you!" With which he turned his back on the incident.

CHAPTER
FOUR

It did get sorted out. Slade Bendix got sent to the head and there was talk of a parent having to come up. In the classroom chairs and tables were moved and Roberta found herself with some other children as far from the boy as it was possible to get. Her face and her arm stopped hurting. The lump in her throat went down and she started to think things would get better. But an ache came back when the head came in for a messenger—and no one even glanced in her direction.

After school dinner, though, a much more painful hurt than punching came her way.

It was only over not knowing how Mr

Ransom liked things done. Did you put a
date on your work? was all she needed to
know. Everyone else had their heads down
doing different things and she'd got a handwriting poem to copy. So did she date it? It
was a normal sort of question and she put
up her hand.

The room was quiet. Slade Bendix was out of the class in his reading group and everyone else was getting on. Mr Ransom was doing the totals in his register—and Roberta Richards put up her hand.

"And what does Madam want?" he asked her.

It was like being ducked in a bath of cold water. It was a heart stopper. It froze the face like a mask and dropped the pen from the hand. It took her breath away. *Madam.*

She'd got to spend all her weekdays till next July with this teacher and he was calling her "Madam" the way he called Slade Bendix "Trouble". Not "Tiddler" or "Jester" or "Princess", like some of the others. But "Madam". It was just in a different language to anything she'd ever been called at Regent.

Somehow she managed to ask her question and she got a straight answer. But after that for some reason her handwriting took on a slope it had never had before.

CHAPTER
FIVE

It hadn't been heaven in Deptford. But Roberta had grown up there in a street full of people who knew her and her family, and had done since she was born. She'd never had to give her name or explain herself to anyone. And at Regent Primary where she'd also grown up she hadn't been called a name to upset her since she'd pushed the wrong pram in the nursery. She was who she was. She wasn't any "Madam" nor anything else with a label, except Roberta Richards from Flat A, 124 Tunnel Street.

Now the address was different, and the people were new, and the way home from school was a lonely new walk. Or rather a run: and she wasn't giving anyone a chance to go with her, even if they'd wanted. All she wanted was home. She got to the juniors' gate in Borden Road, ran three sides round the school and brought herself out in Clipper Street, where the parents were waiting with their push chairs and cars. From there, with the new house pretty well in her sight, she'd only got to put on a spurt to get to the door.

Her mother was in, she knew. "Resting" from acting: out of work for a bit. Which was good news today because Roberta couldn't wait to see a kind face—just someone who knew her real name. She ran past the shop, came to the pub, and started thinking already of the hug she'd get. Then it'd be half an hour's violin, and arrange her room the way she wanted it.

Which was just about all she had left of last night's good feelings: and something she needed now like a body needs food.

The "Yard Arm", squeezed in where two houses would have been, wasn't open yet. There wasn't a sign of life as she ran to it. The picnic table looked sad: just rings on it where the drinks had been, and London dust. But Roberta wasn't interested in that. She hardly gave it a glance, till:

"Pouf!" Slade Bendix had sprung from nowhere. Suddenly he was up on the pub table, pulling a face and starting to mime a mad violinist. He stuck his backside out, closed his eyes, and as he sawed away he gave a raucous "Here we go, here we go!" with his mouth.

But Roberta could ignore all that. He was jealous, that was all, and mad at getting into trouble. She went running on—as the boy suddenly changed his tune and turned his dance into a monkey's, doing the jungle noises Roberta had heard her dad swear at on television football.

Top speed or not there was the time for it to hurt; like a bullet. She ran blindly on and within seconds was at her front door, knocking it down like the last barrier between home and the hyenas of hate.

"Good God, girl, what's this?" her mother wanted to know. But it was a full five minutes before the sobbing and the hiccups stopped and the story of that awful day could come stuttering out.

"It's growing up, my girl, and it's a hard old lesson. Don't I know!" Lucy Richards was crying, too, and her eyes said she would gladly have gone on bearing the hurt for the two of them, if it were possible. "Only we've all got to learn it. We can't kid

41

ourselves things are any different."

Roberta was cried out and shocked out. She was curled up weak and limp in a corner of their old settee, listening to this talk coming at her as if she were suddenly somebody different. She was more like Clarice, getting it straight. She looked at her mother. The mauve make-up round her eyes was worn through and her own happy first-day face had been well wiped off.

"Oh you should see 'em when I go to the

studio all done up. It's 'Hi, Lucy! How you goin'? Good to see you workin'.' Then I get in that make-up overall, scarf on my head and don't look the actress. And I tell you, I

come out of that room for a cup of tea—
and suddenly it's no doors held open any
longer. No 'Lucy' no more. They just
stare, and you can see 'em thinking *Where's
she going? Who's that woman think she is?
What's cleaners doin' up here?*"

Roberta stirred a bit. But she didn't
really get it. They hadn't called her mother
"Madam" and made jungle noises at her,
had they? She hadn't suddenly been moved
out of Regent and into this horrible school
round here.

"Just don't depend on them for what you
think of yourself, is what I'm saying. It's
got to come from you. Don't fit into someone else's image to please 'em. Bring out
your *pride*." Lucy Richards thumped her
own chest with the butt of her hand.
"Someone does that jungle filth to you,
think of 'em as cats miaowing or dogs
barking. They're no more'n animal noises in
the street. An' you just go on walking past
a bit taller than before."

"Yeah...." Roberta said. But she was too played out to think any more. And after a long cuddle she went to bed; straight in, not even wanting to do any arranging of her room.

CHAPTER
SIX

She couldn't face school the next day,
either. She pretended she could. She put
on a brave face and she went: but she
didn't go in. She said goodbye to her
mother at the corner of Borden Street and
when her mother had gone she went right
on past the school as if all she was doing
was running back home for something she'd
forgotten. In the wrong direction—towards
the banks and the restaurants and the
shops and the river.

She kept away from the park. She'd
been warned about parks and people on
their own in them, so she kept with the
crowd and went to the pier and the *Cutty*

was arching behind it in to the pier, lined with people come to see the sights.

She saw a swan being casual and not hurrying out of the way. Roberta watched it to see what would happen. But the swan knew what it was about. It rose on the bow wave and drifted safely away; at home where it was; in control. Not like her any more.

She turned her back on the river, still nowhere special to go, with the emptiness of not having any plan suddenly starting to roll like a hunger in her stomach. She couldn't do this every day till she left school, could she?

It was then that she first saw him: a small boy well under five walking along with great purpose. His face was set and he wasn't hanging about. He was digging in his heels, staring ahead and walking across in front of her. He looked like a toy soldier, only his hands were clutched by his sides and not swinging. As she watched, he marched under the figurehead of the clipper ship and stomped off along the riverside walk. Lucky little devil, she thought. He knew what he was going to do.

The crowd came off the pleasure boat, tans and cameras and plastic macs, and all with those upwards-tilted faces of people who'd come to look about them. Which is why not many of them took any notice of the little boy stomping back from the riverside walk. And stomping in various straight lines across and around the ship and the open space.

But Roberta went on noticing him. She had the time. She saw his straight lines, how he stopped, bewildered, and turned. She saw the look on his face getting tenser and tenser, and she noticed how hard he was clenching those fists.

He's a wound-up toy or he's lost, she thought. *And I reckon I know which it is.*

She'd dealt with all that at Regent in her time. Lost nursery and reception children were nothing new to her. And she knew how sometimes they could hold out and hold out with their eyes all big till they finally gave in and wailed.

She waited till one of his straight lines brought him towards her, when she could crouch down in front of him without a lot of fuss and running.

"You all right, little boy? You lost, are you?"

He looked at her. He stared hard. He narrowed his eyes and set his mouth in a line of closed crinkles. He didn't push past. But he didn't come to her and he didn't say anything. He just stared, and there was no way in the world she could tell what he was going to do.

"You lost, are you?" she repeated.

He went on staring, like a toddler at a cat on the pavement. He might run, he might kick, or he might love.

"Lost your mum, have you?"

But still he stared. Roberta's legs were beginning to ache. You could only do a friendly crouch for so long.

"Come on," she said. "I'll help you find your mum." She held out her arms to pick him up: and with a last, desperate look at her the small boy ran into them and clutched at her. And broke down in the torrent of tears he'd been holding back.

"All right, all right, all right." His gripping hands were hurting her: but he was starting to mumble something in between the sobbing. There was something he was bursting to say.

Roberta listened hard. At first she didn't cotton on; but as he went on gabbling she realised. His crying could have been in English; but the words he was saying were in something else. In something foreign. And the more words he said the more difficult it was to understand him. It was easier in the end when the tears won out.

There was only one thing for it. He couldn't give her any clues so Roberta was going to have to get the boy to a grown-up, to the pier ticket office, or something: but just not to a policeman, if she could help it. She didn't want any awkward questions.

When she went to go, though, she found she couldn't move. He was wailing and clutching at her in his panic at being lost, and it suddenly became clear that she wasn't going to get him anywhere till he was calmed.

CHAPTER
SEVEN

She knew just what do do: what had worked at Regent once or twice. She rocked him in her arms and she sang to him. But she deliberately didn't choose anything with words. Words would only make him feel less at home, she thought, so she chose a tune. Looking up at the tea clipper towering above them she started humming the notes of the violin piece she'd played at the festival, the sea shanty, *Shenandoah*.

And gradually, as she sang the trembling stopped. Not his trembling, but hers—the tremble inside which had started with the

"Madam" and worsened with the monkey dance. The boy's grip loosened and the crying eased. But most of all her throat relaxed and she began to remember who she was.

She was Roberta Richards. A violinist and, by-and-large, a good girl. It didn't matter what anyone thought. It was what she thought that mattered: and she hadn't changed: she was *herself*, because little madams didn't want to help lost boys. And monkeys didn't sing or read music....

Now she could see what her mother had been getting at. Her voice became firmer as she hummed. She had found a lost boy. But most of all she had found that old Roberta Richards again.

Gradually, by not taking things too fast, the boy came with her. She walked him slowly, in time with the sea shanty. He was gripping her hand and looking up at her with trust in his eyes. And Roberta, no longer afraid of what might happen, found

her way through the crowds to a policewoman over by the gangplank to the *Cutty
Sark*.

"Here he is!" the policewoman called
to someone still on the ship. "He...
is ... here." She said some more into her

personal radio: and with a smile for the boy, she took his hand from Roberta's and walked him back over the gangplank to a tanned blond woman in a long raincoat.

Roberta heard the foreign words, and she understood the hug and the tears of the reunion. And she waited for her part to happen. What would the policewoman say to her? *Thank you* or *What were you doing with that boy?*

But what came out was a real shock.

"Roberta Richards?" the woman said. "Come on, my girl, there's a lot of people worried about you, too."

CHAPTER
EIGHT

There were just the four of them outside the headteacher's room. Slade Bendix and his father from the "Yard Arm" pub, Roberta Richards and her mother: with the boy's face still all twisted, and his father caught between two sorts of frown.

"You in trouble an' all?" he asked Roberta, although the question was meant for her mother. "We give 'em too much rope, I reckon."

"Could be," Lucy Richards replied. But she said it the way people agree with a drunk.

"This one's a tyke, I tell you," the man said.

Mrs Richards took a long time replying.
Not in the deciding, but in saying it.

"This one isn't," she told him quietly.

Mr Bendix stared, and nodded. He cros-
sed his legs the other way. But still he
frowned across the space.

"Haven't I seen you somewhere?" he
asked the actress. "Know your face from

somewhere, don' I?" He was smiling a bit. Roberta had seen people do it in shops when they recognised her mother from something they'd seen. It embarrassed her, that smile. She looked away, swung her legs. Next thing they said was, "When you coming on again?"

"Yeah," her mother was saying to the man. "You've seen me. I live up your road."

"Oh," said the publican. "That must be it." He went on looking. "You ever want a little job, bit of cleaning, I'm over the 'Yard Arm'."

"No thanks," Lucy told him.

Roberta looked up at her, saw her straight back and her head held high. She was suddenly very proud of her mum—and all at once aware of how she was sitting herself. Up straight and quite still, she found, and in control; with just the fingers of her left hand moving to the notes of *Shenandoah*.